This is a fable about the hare and the tortoise.

A fable is a story that teaches us how we should behave and how we should treat others. This fable is about a big-headed hare, who thinks he is the best, and his race against the slow-but-steady tortoise.

Here is Hare. He considers himself to be an excellent athlete, who can hop and run very quickly. He is always exercising, doing press-ups and sit-ups, timing himself running, and showing off his muscles.

He never stays long in one place or takes time to sit and think.

Here is Tortoise. He is a strange-looking reptile who carries his home, a shell, on his back. If he is frightened or tired, he just retreats back into his shell.

He never does sit-ups or press-ups, or times himself running, or feels the need to show off his muscles. In fact, he never rushes. He observes life as it goes by him, and thinks hard about things before doing them.

Hare has a favorite running circuit that takes him around a little wood. One day, he set out to run it five times and beat his record.

He was just finishing his third lap, and was checking his time, when he spotted Tortoise sitting there looking at him.

As Hare was finishing his fourth lap, he noticed that Tortoise was still sitting there, under the oak tree, gazing at him. Hare stopped and stared back at Tortoise.

"Are you ill? Are you hurt? Do you need help?" said Hare, puzzled.
"No," replied Tortoise, "I'm just sitting here, thinking. It's a lovely day, isn't it?"
"Are you going to sit there all morning?" said Hare.
"Yes, probably," replied Tortoise, nodding slowly.

Hare shook his head and frowned.
"I don't understand. Why would you just sit there when you could be running, or jumping, or racing?" he continued.
"Well, you just keep running by me. You aren't going anywhere, just zooming around and around in circles. What is the point of that?" said Tortoise.
"Point? Point?" spluttered Hare. "The point is that I win every race I enter. I'm not lazy and slow like you!"

“I challenge you to a race tomorrow morning,” Hare shouted. “Maybe then you’ll see what the point is. We’ll start here and end at the farm.”

Hare loved thinking about the race with the slow old tortoise and he told everyone he met about it. He stayed up late that evening, drinking and joking with his friends. Tortoise, on the other hand, went to bed as soon as it was dark.

The next morning, quite a crowd had gathered to see the strange race. Hare limbered up, stretching and bouncing on his long legs. He ran in circles before the cheering crowd, while Tortoise just sat, and nodded and smiled, waiting for the race to start.

Finally, Fox fired the starting pistol and they were off. Hare soon vanished into the distance, with just a cloud of dust to show where he had been. Tortoise lumbered off, plodding along at a steady pace. He didn't look left or right, just straight ahead, as he determinedly stomped along.

"Go, Tortoise!" shouted many of the other animals. They were trying to be nice and encourage him, while secretly thinking that the race was a bit silly. Of course Hare was going to win!

After his late night, and all the running around and showing off, Hare started to feel tired. Also, as the sun got hotter, it made him feel a bit sleepy. He saw a shady, soft-looking spot under some trees.

"I have plenty of time for a quick snooze. Tortoise will never beat me. It will take him ages to get here," he said to himself. So Hare lay down, just for a little nap, and was soon asleep.

Meanwhile, Tortoise continued plodding, step-by-step, along the track. He enjoyed the feeling of the sun on his shell and sped up as the heat from the sun seeped into his body.

He didn't care if he came first, and he didn't expect to win. He simply wanted to enjoy the day, and his walk. He was determined to finish the race. That was the goal he had set himself.

Around mid-afternoon, Tortoise saw the finish line in the distance. There were a lot of animals there, all peering along the track.
"How nice of everyone to wait for me to finish," smiled Tortoise.

As the line got nearer and nearer he could hear loud cheering, shouting, and clapping. Then, as he crossed the finish line, a cloud of dust appeared in the distance behind him, and Hare came running along the track.

Hare had slept for far longer than he had intended to. When he woke up, he panicked and rushed off, but as he ran over the top of the hill, he could see Tortoise was about to amble over the finish line. "No!" he cried. "This cannot be happening!"

Tortoise was the winner! No one could understand it. Everyone, including Tortoise, was in shock. They clapped him on the back of his shell to congratulate him. They offered him something to drink and put the winner's medal around his neck.

But what had happened to Hare? The animals looked back along the track. Hare finally arrived, panting and sweating as he crossed over the finish line. He sheepishly admitted that he had fallen asleep, and hadn't heard or seen Tortoise stroll by. Hare felt very silly and crept away from the other celebrating animals.

Tortoise smiled and nodded in the middle of all the noise, enjoying the feeling of being the winner. "Rushing around and doing everything as quickly as you can is not necessarily the best way to do things," he told them.

The moral of this fable is that you should always do your best, and that sometimes slow and steady wins the race!